This book is given with love

To:

From:

About the Author

Dr. Daniela Owen is a psychologist who brings to life healthy mind concepts and strategies for children everywhere. For more about the author please check out

drdanielaowen.com

For Lila Skye

 Published in the United States
by Puppy Dogs & Ice Cream, Inc.
ISBN: 978-1-955151-34-4
Edition: May 2021

For all inquiries, please contact us at:
info@puppysmiles.org

To see more of our books, visit us at:
www.PuppyDogsAndIceCream.com

EVERYONE FEELS SAD SOMETIMES

Written by:
Dr. Daniela Owen

Illustrated by:
Gülce Baycik

Sadness can make us feel like a
big, dark cloud is hovering above us.

We may feel sad because
we were left out, we lost a game,
we failed at something we tried to do,
or we couldn't do something that
we really wanted to do.

Sadness may cause us to
stay in bed.

It may cause us to yell
at the people around us.

LEAVE ME ALONE!

Or it may cause us to hide and avoid upsetting thoughts and situations.

Even though it doesn't feel good,
it's okay to feel sad.

Everyone feels sad sometimes...

The good news is, there are things that we can do to make us ***feel happier.***

Ready to hear an important secret?

What we ***do*** changes how we ***feel!***

When we are sad,
doing something that we enjoy and
are good at makes us feel happier.

Try making pipe cleaner animals,
shooting hoops, or creating
an imaginary world to play in.

Another thing that can make us feel happier is doing something kind for someone else.

Try making a homemade card
for a grandparent,
delivering soup to a sick neighbor,
or helping out a friend or sibling.

Dear Grandma,
I love you.
I hope you are having
a good day

When we do something nice
that makes someone else happy,
we feel happy too.

Thank you for the card!
You're welcome!

Here's something else
important for you to know...

What we ***think*** affects how we ***feel!***

THOUGHT

THEN

FEELiNG

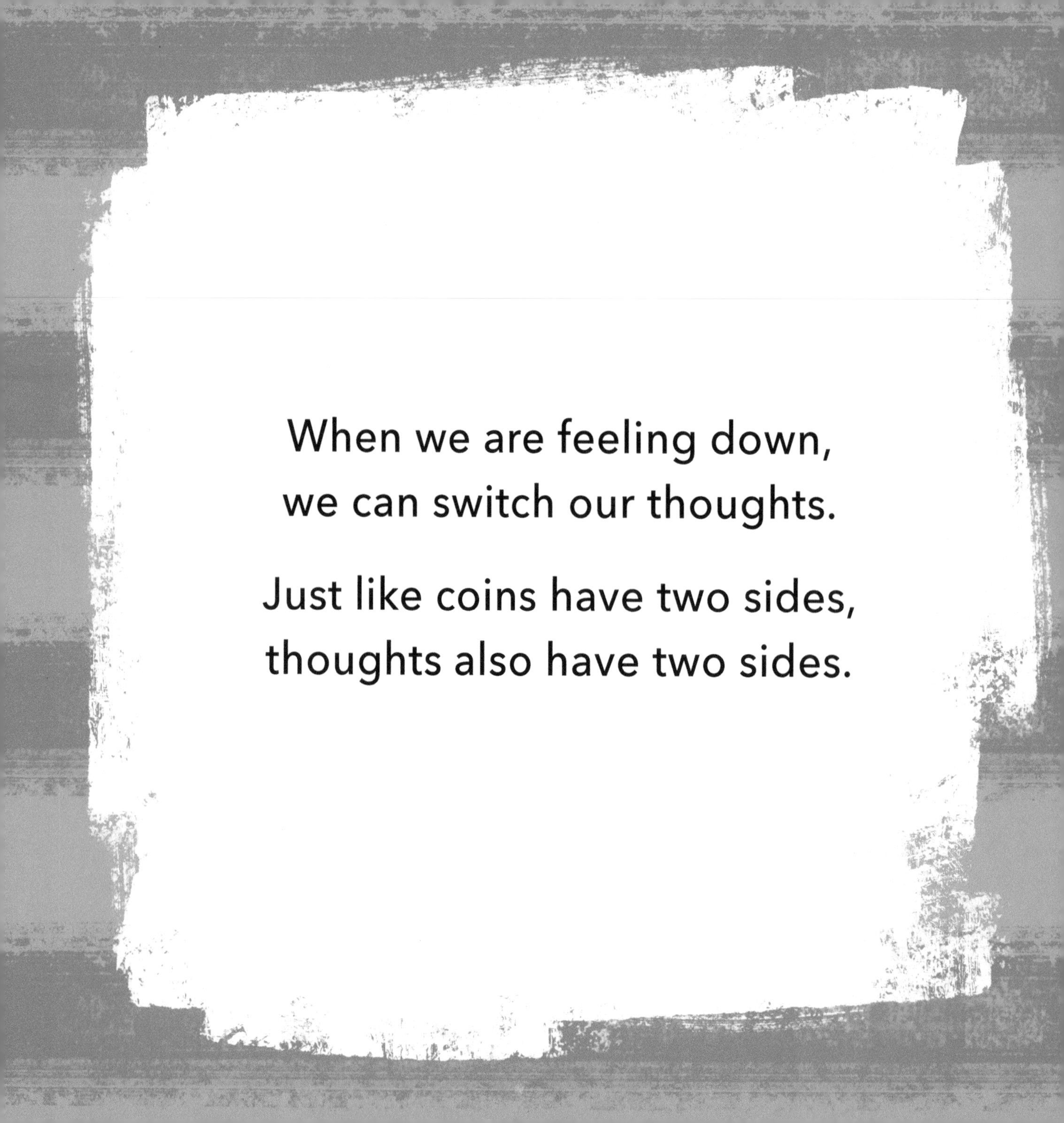

When we are feeling down,
we can switch our thoughts.

Just like coins have two sides,
thoughts also have two sides.

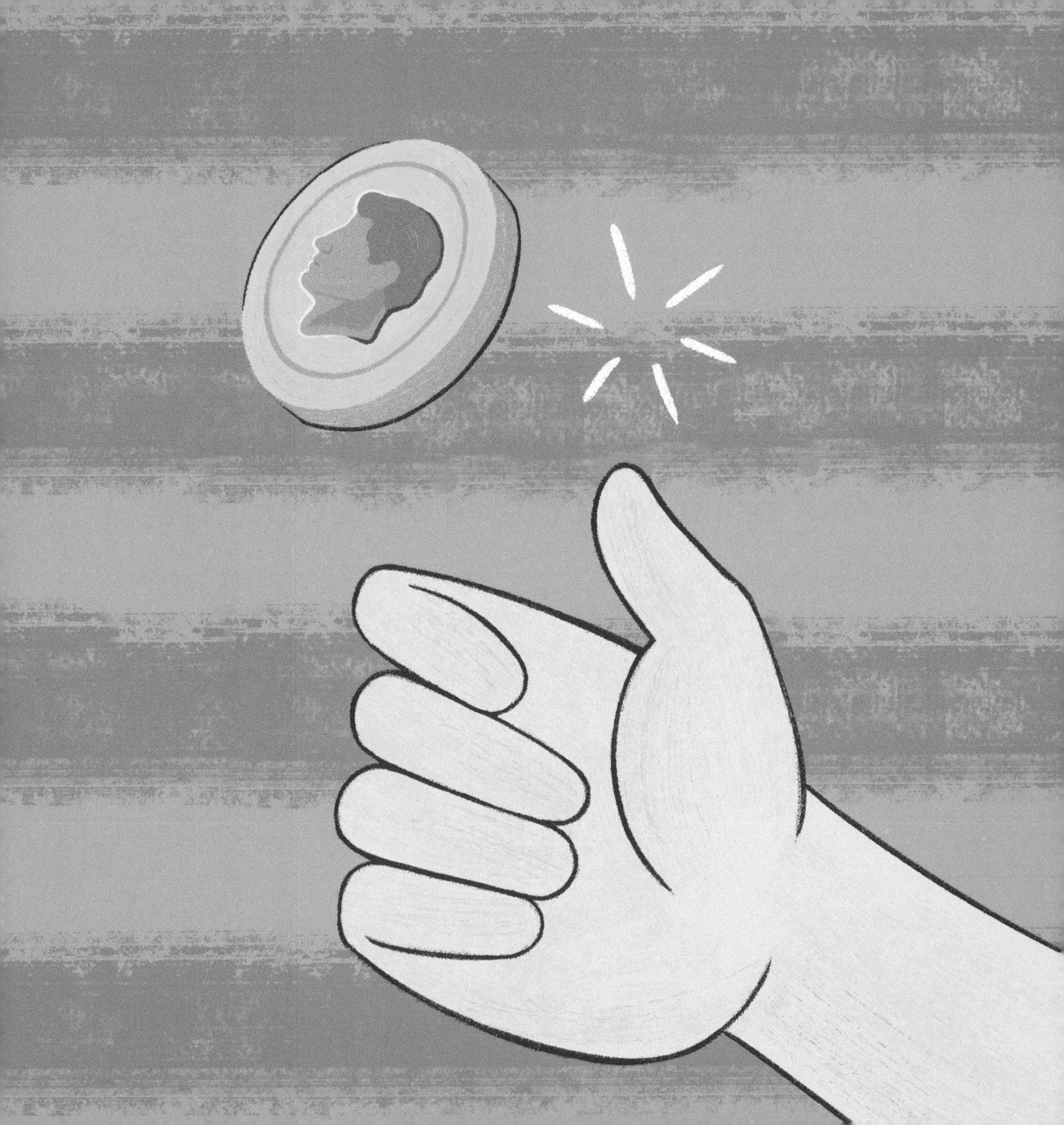

Let's say you have something hard to do.
Your brain might have a thought like,

"This is impossible!
I'll never be able to finish in time!"

I'll never be able to do it!

But you can switch your thought to...

"I can give it a try.
I might be able to do it.
I'll just start and see what happens."

I might be able to do it!

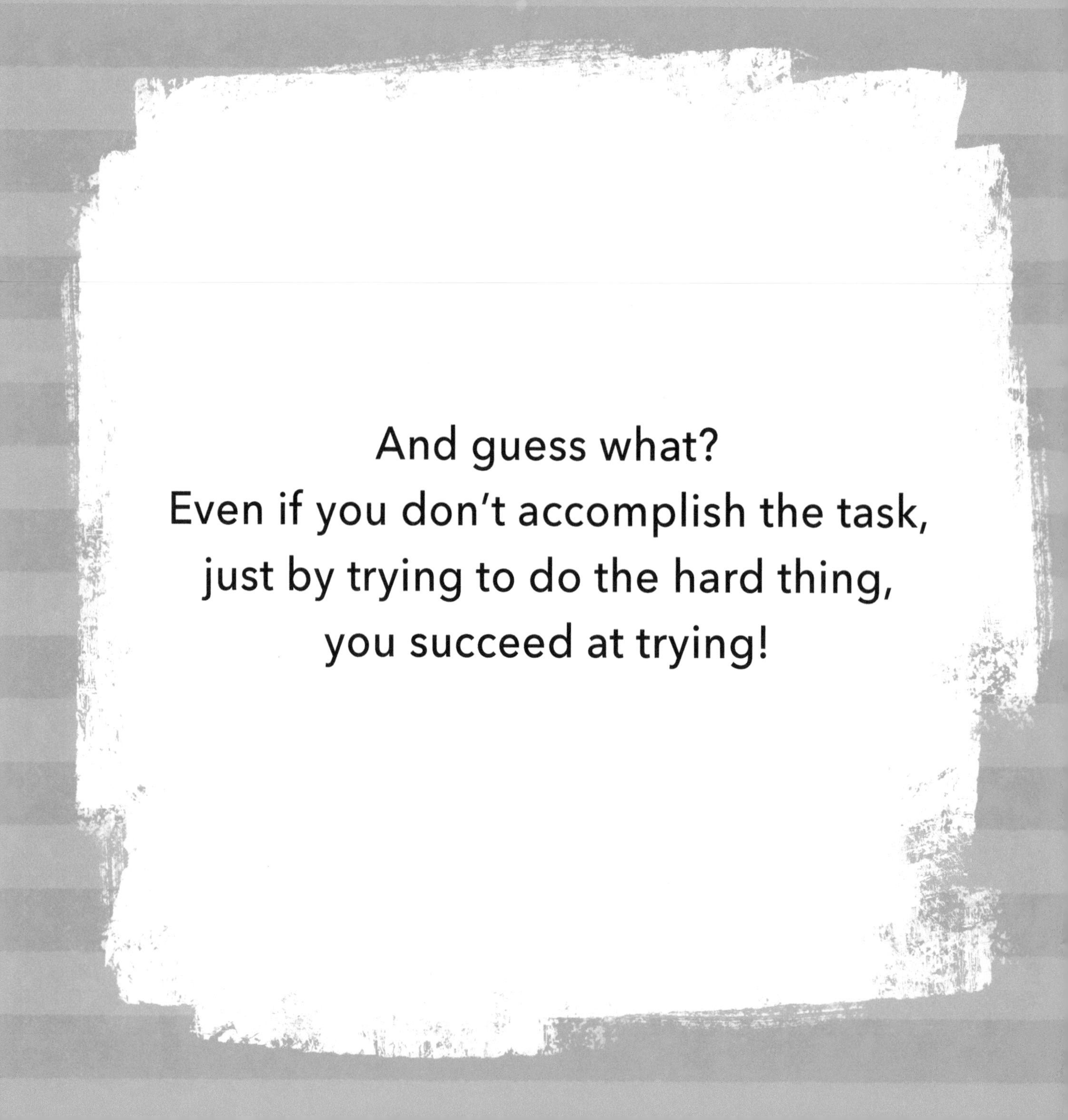

And guess what?
Even if you don't accomplish the task,
just by trying to do the hard thing,
you succeed at trying!

I TRIED

When you succeed,
you should tell yourself,

"I did it!"

Noticing our successes makes us
feel good about ourselves and
makes us want to try again next time.

I DID IT!

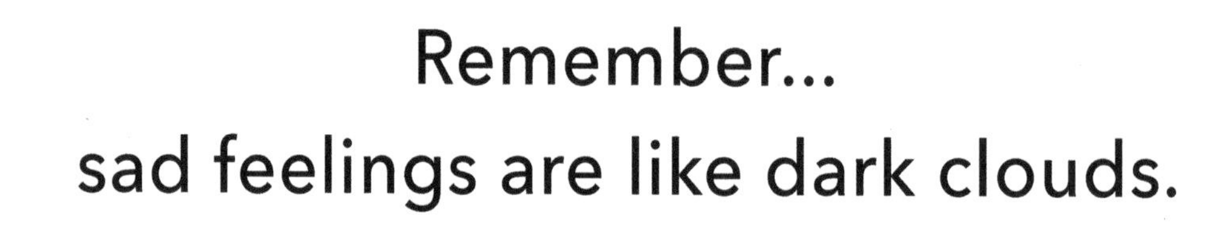

Remember...
sad feelings are like dark clouds.

They always pass by, and
there are sunnier skies ahead!

You have the power to feel happier!

Remember...

Everyone feels sad sometimes!

Turn That Frown Upside-Down!

Fill in the bubbles below with the things you can do to feel happier when you are sad.

Thank you for purchasing

Everyone Feels Sad Sometimes,

and welcome to the Puppy Dogs & Ice Cream family.

We're certain you're going to love the little gift
we've prepared for you at the website above.

CPSIA information can be obtained
at www.ICGtesting.com
Printed in the USA
BVHW061151271022
650468BV00019B/588